2.0 pts
Quiz# 76338

Flight of the Genie

A Magical World Awaits You
Read

THE
SECRETS
OF
DROON

Flight of the Genie

by Tony Abbott
Illustrated by David Merrell
Cover illustration by Tim Jessell

A
LITTLE APPLE
PAPERBACK

SCHOLASTIC INC.
New York Toronto London Auckland Sydney
Mexico City New Delhi Hong Kong Buenos Aires

For Dolores,
the one I love

For more information about the continuing saga of Droon,
please visit Tony Abbott's website at
www.tonyabbottbooks.com

ISBN 0-439-56043-8

Text copyright © 2004 by Robert T. Abbott.
Illustrations copyright © 2004 by Scholastic Inc.

12 11 10 9 8 7 6 5 4 3 2 1   4 5 6 7 8 9/0

Printed in the U.S.A.   40
First printing, January 2004

Contents

One

Footsteps in the Morning

Swish-swish-swish!

Eric Hinkle darted across his friend Neal's patio. He stopped to see if anyone was watching.

"No way," he chuckled. "No one's up yet!"

He stepped onto a lawn chair. Then he braced one leg on the ledge of a window and pulled himself up.

"The things I do for Droon!"

He hooked one heel over the low roof and dragged himself onto the shingles.

"Almost there!" he huffed.

From the moment he had jumped out of bed that morning, Eric knew he had to tell Neal his dream. He couldn't wait until everyone was up. He had to go right then.

And there it was, ten feet away.

Neal's bedroom window.

Eric grinned as he edged across the roof.

Droon was the secret world he and Neal and their friend Julie had found under the basement of his house. When they had dreams about Droon, it meant they were being called to go back.

Droon was a vast land of diamond valleys, floating cities, deep forests, and castles of snow.

It was the home of strange creatures — the six-legged pilkas, the pillow-shaped

Lumpies, the friendly fire frogs, and the Bangledorn monkeys.

Mostly, though, Droon was a place of great people. Eric, Julie, and Neal's best friend there was Keeah, a princess with amazing powers. Magical old Galen was probably the greatest wizard ever known. Max was a friendly, orange-haired, eight-legged spider troll.

Droon was awesome.

But it was a land in trouble, too.

On one side of the world were the Dark Lands of Lord Sparr, a sorcerer as wicked as Galen was good. And there were Ninns, lots and lots of Ninns, Sparr's klutzy red warriors.

There was Kano, a fiery palace; Plud, Sparr's forbidden fortress; and under the Serpent Sea, the mysterious caves of a witch named Demither.

Eric would never forget those caves.

It was deep in Demither's Doom Gate that a jewel called the Red Eye of Dawn was imprisoned. While battling Om, the whispering evil spirit of the Eye, Keeah had saved Eric's life by zapping him with her magic. From that moment on, Eric had his own powers.

It seemed like forever since then, but he had actually counted the days. Eric had been a wizard for exactly one hundred and eighty-seven days.

Eric glanced at his hands.

Zzzz! Silver sparks sprinkled from the tips of his fingers. Practicing what Keeah had told him, he flicked his hand once, and the sparks vanished.

That sort of magic was powerful, but he needed to learn to use his other powers, too. Sometimes he had visions and could hear things no one else could. He had also learned to speak silently to his friends.

Droon had changed Julie, too. Though she didn't have as many magical powers as Eric, on one adventure she had gained the ability to fly!

Tweee! A robin flitted across Neal's roof and vanished into the branches of a tree, chirping its early morning song.

"Right," said Eric. "The reason I'm here. Get ready, Neal. Here comes your wake-up call!"

He braced himself outside the window. Seeing that it was unlocked, he carefully slid his hands under the sash and pulled.

Fooom! The window flew up suddenly.

Eric jerked backward. He grabbed for the sash, missed, slipped on the shingles, and fell.

Right off the roof.

"Hellllllp!" he cried. "Someone — whoa!"

At that instant, two arms slid around

him and lifted him up —all the way back to the roof!

"What? Who? How —"

"Lucky I flew here when I did!"

When he opened his eyes, he was teetering back and forth next to his friend. "Julie!"

She grinned, then shrugged. "At your service."

Eric's heart was pounding like a drum. "Holy cow, thanks, Julie. I had this incredible dream and I needed to tell Neal —"

"Me, too!" she said. "I flew to your room first, but it was empty. I figured you were here."

"Yeah, trying to smush myself!" said Eric.

Laughing, Julie edged to the window. "Time for Neal to wake up. And we'll be his alarm clock!"

The two friends carefully climbed

through the window. Neal lay asleep in his bed, buried in blankets and smiling a big smile.

Eric laughed quietly. "He must be dreaming."

"He's drooling, too," whispered Julie. "So I guess there's food involved. Hey, Neal — *BRRINNG!*"

"Whoa, Mom, I'm coming! Wha —" Neal burst upright, jumped out of bed, and stood wobbling on the floor. He was completely dressed. "What? Who's there? Huh?"

"Neal, wake up. It's us," said Eric.

Sleepily, Neal blinked, finally recognizing his friends. "Oh, man, I dreamed I was playing basketball with a globe of Droon when a bell rang. I thought it meant breakfast was ready."

"We all dreamed of Droon," said Julie. "But, Neal, I have to ask, why do you sleep in your clothes?"

He glanced at his T-shirt and jeans. "So I can get to breakfast faster, of course!"

Eric laughed. "We can get to Droon faster, too. Let's go."

Grinning, Neal opened his bedroom door, looked both ways, then quietly led his friends down the stairs to the living room and out the back door.

As Julie led them across Neal's patio, Eric breathed in the morning air once more.

Having magical powers was great, he thought, but going on an adventure with his friends was really the best part about Droon.

"So tell me your dreams," said Neal as they made their way across his yard.

Chuckling, Eric leaped over a row of bushes. "Mine was all about you. First, you were on a throne in a palace with a giant crown on your head."

Neal nodded. "This is a good thing. I don't know my hat size, but maybe crowns are one-size-fits-all. Go on."

"You looked out at a huge crowd," said Eric. "Then you held up some crusty old scroll. You frowned at it as if it were a math test."

Julie laughed as they sped through Eric's yard. "I know that look. Neal's face wrinkles into a knot!"

"It's all those numbers," said Neal, shivering. "Math is full of them."

"Finally, you nodded and everybody got really quiet," said Eric. "Then you spoke."

Neal stopped. "Really? What did I say?"

"Pointing at the scroll, you said . . . 'I'll have the Droonburger!'"

Neal burst into laughter as Eric opened his back door. "A menu dream. I love those!"

Together, the three friends climbed down to Eric's basement and pushed away two big cartons blocking a small closet door under the stairs.

Piling into the closet, they shut the door, turned off the light, and waited.

Not for long.

Whooosh! The gray floor vanished beneath their feet, and they were standing on top of a staircase shining in every color of the rainbow.

A staircase leading to the land of Droon.

Warm air drifted up from below. It was filled with all the smells of early summer. Birds cooed and chirped gentle songs of morning.

"Guys," murmured Eric. "I have a feeling that today is going to be a great day."

Julie nodded. "Droon adventures are so cool."

"Yeah," Neal agreed. "And I hope our dreams come true, too. I'm planning to order fries with mine —"

But as the friends rushed down the stairs, the birds seemed to stop singing all at once. The breezes stilled. The air went strangely quiet.

Julie slowed to a stop. She looked around. "I guess maybe it's time I told you guys my dream. It wasn't exactly like yours."

"What was it about?" asked Eric.

Rough voices yelled in the distance. Then came the flap of wings and a low growling sound.

Julie gulped. "We were on the stairs. . . ."

Suddenly, the pink clouds parted and the air darkened with a swarm of flying lizards called groggles.

Kaww! Kaww! they shrieked. On the

back of each groggle was a fierce red warrior.

"Ninns!" said Julie. "My dream was about — Ninns!"

"Now you tell us?!" cried Eric.

Thwang-thwang-thwang! A volley of fiery arrows burst across the sky.

"This is not a good thing!" cried Neal.

The Ninns shot another round of flying arrows, and the three best friends tumbled down the rainbow stairs.

Two

Over the Saladian Plains

Clink! Blang! Plink! The arrows hit the stairs.

"Why couldn't you dream of me like everyone else?" cried Neal as he fell down the steps.

"Sorry —" yelled Julie, tumbling faster and faster.

As the three friends toppled head over heels, the rainbow stairs began to wobble.

Laughing, the Ninns drew their bows for another attack.

"Help!" yelled Eric as the stairs began to fade.

Suddenly, a strange sound pierced the air.

Yip-yip-yip!

The clouds parted and a small four-winged airplane looped through the sky — *voooom!*

It flew under the groggles, scattered them, and — *thwoo-oo-oop!* — scooped Eric, Julie, and Neal right into an open compartment on its back.

"Wha —" cried Julie.

Slank! A see-through ceiling closed over them.

A moment later, the plane lifted, tilted, then shot between two snowy peaks, leaving the shrieking groggles and Ninns in its wake.

"What just happened?" asked Neal.

"I think we got rescued," said Julie.

Eric's heart was pounding again. "That's my second time today!"

Just then, a small hatch opened onto the compartment. In popped a big face with a pug nose and a thatch of wild orange hair.

"Max!" cried Julie, jumping to him.

The spider troll laughed brightly. "Welcome to the new, improved *Dragonfly*, Keeah's plane! Good thing we came along when we did. Hee-hee! Follow me!"

As the plane rose and turned, the children followed Max through a narrow passageway to the little plane's cockpit. At the wheel was a young girl with long blond hair.

"Keeah!" said Eric. "We were smushed for sure. Boy, are we lucky you found us!"

The princess smiled. "Too bad the

Ninns found you first. I sure hope we lost them."

"Ho-ho!" laughed a deep voice. "I wonder if we shall ever lose the Ninns!"

Sitting in the back, surrounded by mounds of curled papers, was the wizard Galen. Beside him on a small desk, lying drooped and still, was Quill, the magical feather pen.

"I suspect dreams brought you?" said the wizard, pushing aside a pile of papers so they could sit.

"Cool dreams, mostly about me," said Neal.

Keeah set the controls of the plane to fly by itself, then turned her seat as the children quickly described their dreams.

"Eric dreamed of Neal," said Julie, "and Neal dreamed of himself, playing basketball with a globe of Droon. I dreamed about Ninns attacking us on the stairs."

Galen stroked his beard. "Dreams and memories do sometimes become very real. We shall see more of that today, I think. Keeah, the bottle!"

On the desk next to Quill stood a small bottle made of dark glass. Deep designs coiled over it.

The kids recognized the bottle as the one given to them by the mysterious Prince of Stars.

"The prince said this bottle would be useful against Lord Sparr," said Keeah, giving it to the old wizard.

"But not in the way we'd expect," remembered Julie.

It was clear to all of them that Sparr had a scary new mission. He was bringing together the three greatest objects of power from all over Droon.

"What this bottle has to do with Lord Sparr is not clear," said Galen, running his fingers over the bottle's designs. "But Quill did his best to translate these strange marks for us."

The plane dipped closer to the ground.

"The bottle is very old," said Keeah, reading Quill's papers. "It is called the Bottle of Ut."

Neal blinked. "The bottle of *nut*?"

"No, Ut!" Max laughed. "According to the words, we must take the bottle to a giant sand dune in the Saladian Plains and — *pfft!* — out of it will come . . . the city of Ut!"

The children stared at the dark bottle.

Julie frowned. "There's a whole city in there?"

"There is," said Galen. "Every one hundred years, Ut appears for a single day, then returns to the bottle. Today is that day. But that is not the most remarkable thing. Here." He tapped the marks. "It says that someone is trapped in the city. Someone by the name of . . . *Hoja*."

"Hoja?" cried Eric. "We know him!"

Hoja was the Seventh Genie of the Dove. He wore a giant turban and spoke odd, funny sayings. The kids had met him on an earlier adventure.

"Wait a second," said Neal, raising his hand. "You said that Ut appears once every hundred years. Well, we saw Hoja a little while ago. How could he be trapped in the bottle?"

Max laughed. "Because he is a genie! Genies move through time as much as they like. Hoja must have gone back to Ut the last time it was out of the bottle."

"And he got stuck there when it returned to the bottle?" asked Julie. "Wow."

"Got stuck," said Galen. "Or got captured. Quill has written that Ut is 'a city of dangers.'"

"He also told us to watch for the 'blue flower,'" added Max.

"Blue flower, city of dangers — what does all this have to do with Sparr?" asked Eric. "He already has his Coiled Viper and Golden Wasp. His other great Power, the Red Eye of Dawn, is sealed away halfway across the world."

Galen gazed out the plane's windows. "True," he said. "Ut is a Droon mystery. We must use our powers, all of them, to reveal what new evil Sparr has in mind. For now, our mission is clear. Rescue Hoja before Ut vanishes again!"

"A Droon mystery," said Eric. "Okay . . ."

"Look!" cried Max. "Quill is writing again!"

Scritch! Scratch! The feather pen wiggled quickly on the paper.

"Is Quill writing the future?" asked Julie. "He's writing very fast."

Normally, the magical pen wrote everything that happened in Droon. But sometimes he wrote so quickly that his words were about things that hadn't happened yet.

Quill flopped over, and Galen read the words.

Fly me up, you flying dove,
Fair as the moon, the one I love.

"What does *that* mean?" asked Neal.

Galen stroked his beard, then laughed.

"Silly Quill! This has little to do with Hoja or Ut, or even the future. Quill remembers a poem I wrote a long time ago. About a person I loved. She swept me off my feet, you could say!"

"She?" Max giggled as the plane dipped again. "How did she ever put up with you?"

The wizard laughed again. "I ask myself that all the time!"

The tall grass and rolling dunes of the immense Saladian Plains spread before them as the *Dragonfly* flew lower.

"Get ready, everyone," said Keeah, sliding into the pilot's seat. "We're going down there."

The princess pulled on the wheel, and the plane slowed and thudded down, sending waves of sand high up behind it. Flapping its wings one last time, the small craft came to a stop.

"We must set the bottle in the center of the great dune," said Max, holding it carefully.

"Maybe we should bring Quill, too?" asked Neal. "He might help us find where Hoja is."

"Good idea." Keeah stuffed a pad of paper and the feather in her belt. Quill wiggled once, then fell asleep.

When the small crew stepped out of the plane, heat poured up all around them. Almost instantly, funnels of sand spun here and there from the dunes.

"Should we blast those away?" asked Eric.

Keeah shook her head. "I'm learning other powers. *Sofo . . . la . . . koom!*"

Fwoosh! Instantly, the funnels settled down.

Neal smiled. "Now, that is a very good thing."

"It comes!" Galen walked up to the top of the sand dune. The misty pink clouds of early morning were just giving way as the great Droon sun rose over the mountains.

"The sky turns sapphire blue," he said.

"The sun shall strike the exact spot. Max, quickly now!"

Max scampered up the dune and planted the bottle in its center.

For a moment, everything seemed to pause.

The plains were silent and still.

All of a sudden, the sun's rays burst through the morning clouds and slanted across the earth until they struck the dune. The bottle began to shake.

"Awesome!" whispered Julie.

"The adventure begins once more," said Galen. "How I wish I could do this for-ever!"

"And me with you!" chirped Max.

All at once — *whooooomf!* — thick, purple smoke shot out of the bottle. It blew upward in great, billowing puffs around the children.

Eric found himself staring, astonished, as the whole world of sky and sun and sand gave way to a giant city.

"Behold!" cried Galen, raising his arms in the air. "The city of Ut comes again!"

Three

In the Streets of Ut

"Look, everyone!" gasped Max. "Oh, look!"

Out of the spinning purple smoke, rose shapes.

First one wall sprouted from the empty sands as if it were alive. Then came a great curved tower, then a twisted dome. One after another, buildings rose up magically.

It was as if every shape and turn of the

smoke suddenly hardened into solid purple clay when touched by the sun.

At last, a great rolling wall surrounded everything. Then came a deep and booming shudder, and the purple city stopped rising.

Julie gasped. "The city of Ut! It's really real!"

Almost instantly, the noise of crowds yelling and pilkas whinnying drifted over the walls.

"It's real, all right," said Neal. "Real bad. I'm not liking it so much. Too . . . weird looking."

"Quill doesn't like it, either," said Keeah, holding up the pad of paper as Quill wiggled wildly, then stopped. "He just wrote, *black nets*. Quill? Quill! He fell asleep again."

"Perhaps he does write about what is to

come," said Galen, breathing heavily. He led the little troop quietly across the sand to the giant wall. "Ut is indeed a mystery, my friends. We may need Quill's clues today, for trapped somewhere in this city is a friend."

Stopping at the foot of the wall, Eric placed his hand on the purple clay. It was rough and hard and already soaking up the heat of the day.

"We need to be careful here," he said, "and not give ourselves away. We should probably keep our magic quiet until we need it."

"Good idea," said Keeah. "And keep ourselves quiet, too. Come on, everyone." Grasping a curved space in the wall, she lifted herself up and started to climb. Galen and Max went next, followed by Julie, Neal, and finally Eric.

Seeing all his friends clamber up the

wall above him, Eric couldn't help but smile. He thought of climbing up to Neal's roof that morning.

And here he was again.

Sneaking into a city with a genie trapped inside. Ut was a mystery, all right. And if Sparr were involved, it would certainly be dangerous. And full of adventure. And exciting.

But that was why he loved Droon.

Ten minutes later, they reached the top of the wall together.

"Oh, my gosh!" whispered Julie.

Below them was a world of the strangest buildings they had ever seen. Shops and houses leaned this way and that over narrow alleys filled with amazing creatures.

There were little furry bundles in colored robes scurrying from one corner to the next. Tall green creatures with long

arms and legs rode down cobblestone lanes on trotting black pilkas.

There were large dog-headed beasts here and there, too. They carried big black nets on the ends of long poles.

"Guards with black nets," whispered Julie. "Just like Quill said."

"Then let us enter silently," said the wizard. "If I remember correctly, dogs have good ears!"

Without speaking, the small band hopped from the wall to a high, slanted roof. They slid down one roof after another until they finally dropped into an alley between two rows of short buildings.

Looking both ways, Keeah darted to the end and peered around the corner. After a moment, she called her friends over, one by one. Together, they crept to the next street, careful to stay in the shadows.

At an outdoor counter ahead of them,

Eric noticed knobby-skinned creatures wrapping what looked like fruit in crinkly silver paper.

Next door to that was a crooked little shop that smelled like cheese. Nearby, dozens of sausages hung from the ceiling of a yellow awning. Hunks of bread were piled on low tables beneath.

"This is awesome," said Julie.

"Breakfast!" shouted a voice. "One sneddle!"

Neal tugged Galen's cloak. "Um . . . that guy said breakfast. I never got breakfast this morning."

"Do not attract attention, Neal," said Galen.

But before they could slip away, an orange chipmunklike creature poked its head out of the shop, spotted Neal, and blinked. "One sneddle for breakfast, but for you — free!"

Neal grinned at his friends. "What is Quill talking about, 'city of dangers'? City of chow, maybe. Food is definitely the international language! I'll just be a second. And I'll come back with enough for everybody!"

"Neal —" said Keeah. "Neal, be careful!"

He gave a little wave and quietly entered the store.

Keeping an eye on Neal, the rest of the group walked on. Streets twisted and crisscrossed far into the distance.

"How are we going to find Hoja in all this?" asked Eric. "Ut is huge. I already feel lost."

Taking out a small, curved telescope, Keeah gazed through the crowd. "I see a building two streets ahead that has thick bars on the windows."

"Bars?" said Max. "Maybe Hoja really *is* being held prisoner."

Galen smiled. "It will be good to see our friend again —"

He stopped. His eyes were fixed on the crowd moving past the corner ahead. "But wait. Look there! There!"

Max stared where Galen was pointing. "Is it Hoja? Do you see him?"

Without answering, the wizard bounded out of the shadows.

"Galen?" said Keeah. "Wait —"

Galen whisked through the crowded street, turned, paused, then flew around the corner.

"Was it something we said?" asked Julie.

"But we didn't say anything!" said Max.

"Maybe he saw Hoja," said Keeah. "Let's go."

Even as they rushed after him, Eric saw Galen point into the crowd ahead. Someone in a white robe flashed by, turned, then disappeared in the crush of people.

"Galen's after someone," Eric whispered. "Hurry up!"

Together, they charged ahead, not daring to call Galen's name, but rushing after him as quickly as he followed someone else.

"He went in here," said Keeah, running into a stable of pilkas.

The steaming breath of the animals and the smell of straw mixed with an almost sweet smell. But the wizard was nowhere to be seen.

Julie called out, "Galen! Where are you —"

"We'd better get back to Neal," said Eric.

Keeah stopped short.

"What is it?" asked Max.

"The square," she said. "Look!"

The far end of the stable opened onto a large square filled with people. In the exact center of the square was a huge design made of bright blue tiles. The design was in the shape of a blue flower.

"Blue flower," whispered Eric. "It's just what Quill wrote!"

"Guards," said Julie.

"He didn't write anything about guards," said Max.

"No, I mean — *guards*!" cried Julie.

Suddenly — "*woof-woof!*" — a troop of armor-wearing dog-headed guards bounded down the street, barking loudly. They marched heavily on thick, furred feet. Above their heads, they twirled oversize black nets.

"Quickly, into the shadows!" hissed Max. "Let the guards pass —"

But the guards didn't pass. They came to a sharp halt.

A big golden carriage pulled by two black pilkas rumbled up behind them and slowed.

As the kids watched — *swoosh!* — curtains on the carriage parted and a shiny metal hand came out. It was a glove made of silvery iron.

"HALT!" shrieked a voice from inside the carriage.

The carriage's wheels scraped the cobblestones as it ground to a stop.

Everyone froze in the streets, waiting.

The curtains opened further and a boy's head came thrusting out into the sunlight.

Eric staggered on his feet.

The boy's hair was piled very high on his head. He wore narrow green glasses. He had little pink roses painted on his cheeks. His mouth was screwed up into a snarling frown.

But there was no mistaking his face.

Eric knew that face.

It was the face of his oldest friend.

"N-N-Neal? Is that you? We left you getting food. How did you —"

The boy glared at Eric. He wrinkled his nose to match his snarling mouth. "Neal? NEAL? I am not Neal! I am Duke Snorfo, Ruler of Ut! And *you* — are under arrest!"

Four

A Dungeon with a View

Eric stared at the boy. "You're not Neal?"

Keeah frowned. "He's not Neal?"

"He sure looks like Neal," said Julie.

The boy's eyes turned icy. "I'm not —
NEAL!" he shrieked, his face turning as
purple as the walls. "GUARDS! Take them
you-know-where!"

A dog-headed creature bowed low.

"Which dungeon, Duke Snorfo? The dark one or the smelly one?"

The boy grinned cruelly. "YOU decide!" Then he turned to Julie and grunted. "And you — Dumpella — get in the carriage. It's a BIG DAY!"

Julie stepped back and blinked. "Me? Dumpella?"

"I see you've been shopping for silly clothes again, sister!" he snarled. "You'll soon be back in your royal robes. Now, GET IN!"

Clink-clank! The boy snapped the fingers of his iron glove and the guards pushed Julie right into the duke's carriage.

"See you later, *prisoners!*" said the boy. Then he chuckled. "NOT!"

Clop-clop-clop! Eric got a last glimpse of Julie's face as the black pilkas reared and the duke's carriage sped away across the tiled plaza.

Before they knew it, the troop of dog-headed guards dropped their big black nets over the three friends, hustled them to the building with bars on the windows, dragged them down ten flights of stairs, and heaved them through a metal door at least a foot thick.

Thump — thump — thump!

Max moaned as he rolled over the floor. "Is this the dark dungeon or the smelly one?"

The chief guard barked, "A little of both!"

"Don't just visit," said another. "Stay a while!"

The dog-headed troop woofed and huffed, then trotted out of the small stone room and slammed the door behind them — *clang-g-g-g!*

The sounds of the guards' feet echoed up the stairs. A moment later, they were gone.

Max gulped. "So . . . that wasn't Neal?"

Keeah looked around at the stained walls. "No. I think we found Neal's evil twin. I mean, Neal may be nutty, but he's not crazy."

"Except maybe about food," said Eric, slumping to the floor. "And that's what probably saved him. I can't believe it. In, like, a minute, we lose Julie, Neal, and Galen, and then we get plunked into a dungeon. . . ."

Max rubbed his head. "A dungeon that will soon be sucked back into a bottle for a hundred years!"

"Thanks for reminding me," said Eric with a sigh. "We're here to rescue Hoja. But who will rescue us?"

"No one," said Keeah, staring at some marks on the wall. "At least not here. These are messages from people who spent time in this cell."

Eric and Max jumped up and began to read.

"*A hundred years! No escape!*" read Max. "This is not, as Neal would say, a good thing."

"But look at this one," said Keeah. "*Was here ten minutes, then found a way out. If you're trapped — dig down — through the floor! Bye!*"

Eric laughed. "Yes! Someone escaped! Whoever it was, dug down. There must be a tunnel under the floor!"

They searched the floor of the dungeon. In one of the corners they found a large stone raised a little higher than the rest of the stones. It looked as if it had been moved.

"This is it!" said Eric. "Whoever wrote that note dug down under this stone. It's heavy. Stand back, everybody!"

"Eric, I don't know —" Keeah started.

Mumbling some words, he aimed his fingers at the stone. A bright silver beam shot out the ends of his fingers. *Zzanng! Blam! Boom!*

The spray of sparks bounced off the stone and shot back up, zigzagging from one wall to the other and sending the kids flying for cover.

"Eric!" cried Keeah, diving over Max.

Ping! Blam! Boom! Sparks blasted the stones with deep, fiery marks wherever they hit.

Finally, the light faded, and the friends were left cowering in the dim stone room once more.

"Uh, sorry about that," said Eric. "I have a better idea. Maybe we should just, you know, dig?"

Keeah gave him a look, then smiled. "Dig."

Scrabbling and scratching together, the

three friends dug around the stone and managed to lift it.

Underneath, dug into the earth, was a hole.

"A tunnel," said Max. "And a way out!"

They dropped into the hole and scraped along a narrow tunnel. First they went downward, then sharply upward. Finally, they saw an outline of light around a rock blocking the tunnel.

Pushing the rock forward, they followed it into a room larger and lighter than the first.

"We made it!" cried Eric.

Looking around, he saw a barred window high near the ceiling. In one corner was a heap of dirt. In another was a pile of rags. Mostly there was stone.

Except for the walls.

They were made of metal.

"We made it," said Keeah, running her

hands over the slippery metal. "But I don't know about these walls. You can't climb them. Even if we could, it's a long way up. A long way . . ."

"And the window's got bars," added Eric.

Max frowned. "But where's the door? I wanted a door. I see no door —" His tiny shoulders drooped, and he cried out, "This isn't the way out! This isn't even the way *in*. This isn't the way anywhere!"

"Humf!" growled a voice. "I wish someone had told *me* that before I dug through sixty feet of rock!"

Five

At the Drop of a Pickle

Eric jumped. The pile of rags in the corner rolled, stretched wide, then stood upright.

Before them stood a man. A very short man. He wore tattered pants that billowed like sails and a stained yellow robe. He had a scruffy beard and a shiny, bald head. His eyes blinked once, twice, three times at the light.

"Welcome. I am Hoja, Seventh Genie of the . . . Wait a second — I know you!"

The genie smiled broadly as Keeah, Eric, and Max started jumping up and down.

"Hoja!" cried Keeah. "Oh, my gosh! Yes, it's us. I can't believe we *found* you!"

"It was you who wrote that message!" chirped Max. "We came to Ut to rescue you!"

"Yes, I wrote the note!" said Hoja. "Yes, you found me. Now all we need is for someone to find *you*. Because, my friends, we're trapped!"

Everyone stopped jumping.

Eric grumbled. "Right. We're trapped. But you're a genie, right? You're the Seventh Genie of the Dove. Can't we just fly out of here?"

Hoja smiled sadly. "We *should* just fly

out of here. But I would have already done that if I could. Do you notice anything missing? Besides a door, that is?"

Keeah gasped. "Your hat!"

Hoja nodded. "When I was captured, Duke Snorfo took my very large and excellent turban away from me. I used to go anywhere. I could even walk through walls. Now watch this —"

Hoja marched toward the wall. *Wham!* He smashed right into it and rubbed his nose. "I was sent here to find a genie named Anusa who got stuck in Ut a hundred years before me. Then, look what happened. I myself get stuck . . . oh!"

The floor swayed suddenly and began to rumble. It lasted for a few seconds, then stopped.

"What was that?" asked Eric.

Hoja shrugged. "Just one of Ut's fun little problems. The rumbling keeps getting louder, but it can't shake down these walls!"

"Maybe Quill can tell us the way out," said Keeah. She pulled the pen and paper from her belt. The feather pen shook once, then scribbled.

Max read from the paper and snorted. "'The flower that booms'? Our magical friend can't spell. It should be 'the flower that *blooms*.' Besides, we already found the blue flower in the square. Quill?"

But the pen had already begun snoring.

"Great time for a nap," said Eric. "We're locked up. Half our people are lost who knows where. The earth is quaking. There's a crazy duke in charge. And Ut is just waiting to go slurping back into a bottle for a hundred years!"

"It doesn't look good," said Hoja. "But a wise man once said, 'If you're trapped — dig down!'"

"Sorry, Hoja, you were the one who said that," said Keeah. "And we already tried it."

"Oh," he said. "Well, that didn't work, did it? Still, genies are usually quite clever. We ought to be, we live forever."

"Really?" asked Max. "You live forever?"

Hoja nodded. "I'm the Seventh Genie of the Dove, but the first six are still around somewhere — or sometime. When we get old, we get very old. Then we are called on a journey. Then we get reborn! It's quite nice, actually. Doesn't do a bit of good now, though!"

As the ground shook again, Eric dropped to the floor with a thud. When he did, he saw deep marks scratched into the stones. "What's all this?"

The genie sighed. "A map of Droon. I doodled it from memory. There's not that much to do in here."

Eric stared at the shapes of the valleys, mountains, and seas. He ran his fingers from the wide Saladian Plains, where they were now, all the way across the world to the Serpent Sea, where he had gotten his powers.

"Powers," he mumbled. "I wish I could —"

Plumf! Something fell on the stones next to his foot. He looked at it.

It was a pickle.

Eric swallowed. "Um . . . who dropped a pickle? I mean, who even *has* a pickle?"

"Excuse me," said a distant voice. "If some food fell down there, can you brush it off and toss it back up?"

Everyone looked up. There was a face in the tiny window above them.

Hoja hissed. "It's Duke Snorfo. Hide —"

"Hide?" snapped Max. "We're already in a dungeon!"

It was that same face as before.

A face they knew.

But when Eric stared at it, he saw the mouth move. It was chomping up and down.

On a sandwich.

Eric began to smile. "That's not Duke Snorfo. It's Neal! The *real* Neal! Hey! It's us! Neal! Help!"

Their friend jumped as he grinned down at them. "No wonder you guys weren't around when I looked for you. Hey, you found Hoja!" He pulled on the window bars. "These are thick, but somebody gave me a pet pilka and a rope. We'll have you out of there in no time. Just bring my pickle!"

Tying one end of a stout rope to the bars, Neal fastened the other around his pilka's back. Then he gave the pilka a pat.

Hrrrr! It whinnied, then — *krrrr-ploing!* — it pulled the thick iron bars right off the window. Then Neal dangled the rope down into the dungeon.

Within two minutes, the pilka had pulled Keeah, Eric, Hoja, and Max up and out into the sunny street. Scruffing the pilka's nose, Neal gave it a pat and let it go. "Thanks for the help, pal!"

"This is so awesome!" said Keeah, hugging Neal.

"No kidding," said Neal. "I thought I'd lost you forever. And where are Julie and Galen?"

"You almost did lose us," said Max pulling everyone into the shadows. "As for Julie and Galen, you'll never believe it!"

"First of all," said Eric, "Galen took off after some kind of pale ghosty person all in white. And there are rumblings and quakings —"

"But that's not the worst part," chirped Max.

"The duke of Ut looks exactly like you!" said Hoja.

Neal dropped his sandwich. "Like me? No wonder people gave me free food — they must have thought I was him!"

"Plus, he rules with an iron fist," said Keeah.

"So he's tough, is he?" asked Neal, picking up his sandwich again.

Hoja laughed. "No, the duke really has a metal glove he likes to bang on things. He yells a lot, too."

"But that's not the worst part, either," said Max, dusting off Neal's pickle and giving it to him.

"Julie looks *exactly* like his sister," said Eric. "In fact, he dragged her off to his palace!"

"*That's* the worst part," said Max.

"Once the duke realizes it's not her, she'll be in big trouble. Not to mention that we only have a few hours left before — *pfft!* — Ut goes back into the bottle."

Neal nodded as he crunched into the pickle. "We have to save Julie. And find Galen. That's all there is to it."

"And that's the best part!" said Hoja. "The duke took my turban to his Museum of Magic. When I have it back, I'll be all genie again. And I have a feeling we'll need as much magic as we've got to make this crazy mixed-up day come out right!"

"Sounds like a plan," said Keeah, looking up at the sky. "We'd better hurry. It's already afternoon."

"To the Museum of Magic," cried Max, following Hoja down the shadowy street.

"Don't forget me," said Neal, finishing his pickle. "I can probably get us in for free!"

Six

Museum of Magic

Moving quickly through the shadows, Hoja darted into a narrow alley alongside the prison. "We need to stay out of the light," he whispered.

"So we don't get caught," added Max.

"And because without my turban I get sunburned!" Hoja chuckled softly. "This way!"

Eric kept running over in his mind what

had happened. The dreams. The bottle. The duke.

"Galen was sure right about Ut being a mystery. I mean, we found Hoja, but things got way complicated. And Julie and Galen are still gone."

Keeah nodded. "And this rumbling under the ground . . ."

"I know!" said Neal. "I fell twice in the streets before I found you. You don't know how many times that pickle fell before you saw it!"

Eric remembered what had been said about the Bottle of Ut. It would be useful against Sparr.

But not how they expected.

Right now, he thought, *I expect just about anything!*

"There it is!" said Hoja, putting up his hand. "The Museum of Magic. My turban is in there."

They had reached the big, tiled square again. The museum stood nearby like a giant mushroom of purple stone. Two furry guards stood on each side of a high black arch. It looked dark inside the building, but everyone felt they had to go in.

"Maybe we can try an old trick to distract the guards," said Keeah. She picked up a pebble from the street and threw it hard. It hit a distant wall with a loud *smack*.

"Over there!" cried one of the dog-headed sentries, pointing to the nearby alley. The guards rushed off to it.

"Cool move," said Eric. "Now let's go."

Together the small group rushed up the steps, through the arch, and into the cool darkness of the museum.

Inside, they found one corridor after another leading to giant rooms filled with nothing but stolen treasure.

Eric felt his neck tingle as he saw the rows and rows of glass cases holding swords, scrolls, jeweled goblets, and crowns.

In some tall cases stood life-size mannequins wearing beaded robes and winged headdresses. The figures modeling them looked almost alive. One woman wore a mask with two noses. A man next to her had a bushy mustache and a belt hanging with golden pouches.

"Strange stuff," whispered Neal.

"And magical," said Keeah. "All magical."

"My master would love it," said Max quietly. "He would know what everything means."

Eric wished he knew. Looking at all those magical objects, he felt as if he wanted to try them all.

"The magical urns of Parthnoop!" whispered Hoja. He pointed at several large pots standing together. Some were brown, some blue, some green. But all of them were decorated with circles and spirals and other designs. "I've read about these urns. But never mind. I must find my turban!"

Amid the treasures, Eric spotted what he knew right away was an enchanted object.

It was a globe of Droon, obviously made long ago. Eric could tell it was old because it showed great stretches of dark land under the rule of Emperor Ko, the ancient leader of the beasts.

Eric stared amazedly at the globe, not moving an inch.

But the globe did.

It turned slowly in midair, wisps of clouds drifting across its surface like smoke. In the seas that covered half the world, miniature waves splashed and spilled around tiny wooden ships.

It was like watching a movie.

As he stared at it, Keeah came up behind him. "Galen says that when Ko ruled, he was even more powerful than Sparr is today. Almost all of Droon was dark."

He turned to her. "Sparr wants it like that again. That's what he's always wanted."

"We have to hope that we can stop him."

Stop him.

A sudden shiver tingled up Eric's back. Sparr's power was growing every minute. His lands were getting bigger all the time. Did the friends really have the power to stop him?

And what did Ut have to do with it all?

As the globe turned, the southeast of Droon passed before them, showing the Serpent Sea.

"The Doom Gate is there," he said.

"Where the Red Eye of Dawn is. Wher[...]
got my powers —"

"Turban! There you are, my old friend!"
Hoja squealed suddenly.

At the sound of his voice, the genie's
enormous turban, wound of brilliant red
cloth and studded with jewels, burst from
its case. It began zipping around the room
excitedly and singing loudly. *Eee-ooo-eee!*

Too loudly. The sound of stomping feet
echoed down the halls.

"Guards!" hissed Neal. "They hear us —"

The turban let out a sudden shriek and
shot up in the air.

"Get back here! And *shhh*!" said Keeah,
leaping for it. She grabbed the turban, but
it just flew faster, sweeping her up with it
all the way to the ceiling.

"Uh-ohhh!" she cried. The hat spun her
around the entire ceiling twice. Then it
stopped and hovered in the air, quivering

above them. Keeah dangled from the turban by both hands.

Thomp! Thomp! Four furry, dog-
headed guards entered the room.

"Yikes!" Eric ducked under a display
case next to Neal.

Hoja flew into a corner. "Neal, be the
duke!"

"What?" asked Neal, whirling around.
"Me?"

"Just yell a lot!" cried Max, scurrying to
Hoja.

By the time the guards marched over,
Neal was the only one there.

Shivering, but taking a deep breath, he
frowned deeply.

The guards bowed. "Is everything all
right?"

"Perfect," he said. "I mean — PERFECT!"

The guards bowed. "Snorfo!"

"Bless you," said Neal.

Eric whispered up to Neal. "Snorfo is your name!"

Neal blinked. "And what's Julie called?"

"Dumpella," Eric hissed. "Now get the guards out of here!"

Seeing Keeah dangling up near the ceiling, Eric wondered how long she could hold on to the turban.

Neal laughed loudly. "Oh, guards? I'll stay here while you go to the palace cafeteria and grill me a DROONBURGER!"

Eric groaned. "Oh, not more food . . ."

The guards bowed again. "Yes, Duke Snorfo!"

"Medium rare," said Neal.

"Yes, Duke!" The guards turned.

"With a side of fries!"

"Yes, Duke!" The guards marched away.

"Neal, stop it —" whispered Eric.

"And a pickle!"

The guards stopped.

"No . . . no . . ." groaned Eric.

"But . . ." said one guard, "but . . . Duke Snorfo . . . *hates* . . . pickles!"

"Hates pickles?" Neal snorted. "What kind of nut is he? I mean, am I? I mean — never mind. Hold the pickles!"

"You . . . you are not the duke!" the guards barked.

"No, he's not the duke!" shrieked a high voice. "Because — I AM THE DUKE!"

Everyone turned to the museum door where a boy, looking almost exactly like Neal, came stomping into the room.

"I AM DUKE SNORFO!" he cried out.

No one moved. Nothing stirred in the large room.

Until a small piece of paper fluttered all the way down from the ceiling and settled at the duke's feet.

Eric glanced up. As Keeah dangled,

Quill was wiggling against the pad on her belt, its feather swishing and swatting at the princess's nose.

The duke frowned at the paper at his feet, then stooped to pick it up. He read out the words.

"'Whispers of doom,'" he said. "Whispers of doom? What in Droon's name does WHISPERS OF DOOM mean?"

Eric winced. "Uh-oh . . ."

Quill stretched and wiggled in Keeah's face. Once . . . twice . . .

Clack-clack-clack! At that point, a girl dressed in multicolored capes, with brown hair sticking straight out on either side of her head, and big red hearts painted on her cheeks, wobbled into the room on a pair of tall pink shoes.

"Dumpella," said the duke.

Eric gulped from under the display case. "Julie?"

The girl leaned back to see under the case. "Eric?"

"Dumpella!" said the duke.

"Aaaaa — choooo!" Keeah sneezed suddenly. She and the magical turban fell to the floor, landing together with a soft *thump*.

"Guards!" barked the duke.

"*Wooooof!*" barked the guards.

"Run!" cried Hoja, grabbing the turban.

"Yeah, run!" cried Neal.

"Into the urns of Parthnoop!" cried Hoja.

"Yeah, into the urns of — WHAT?"

Clink-clank! The duke snapped his iron fingers.

And the dog-headed guards charged.

Seven

Nose to Nose . . . to Nose

The children, Max, and Hoja popped into the magical urns of Parthnoop.

"Urns of Parthnoop, roll us out of here!" said Hoja. "Please!"

Instantly — *fooom!* — the urns tipped over and sped across the floor, knocking down the guards as if they were bowling pins!

"*Woof-woof!*" More guards charged in from across the room.

"Behind us!" cried Neal.

"In that case," yelled Hoja, wiggling his turban, "Duke Snorfo and all his guards — freeze!"

Kweeeek! At once, the guards and the duke froze in their places, as if they were statues.

The urns rolled to a stop, and the kids slid out.

Everyone rushed over to Julie.

Keeah hugged her. "Are you okay?"

Julie nodded. "Once I get out of these shoes I will be. Oh, but that was weird. I'm so mad at that brother of mine. I mean, of hers. He keeps bossing me around and he's so snotty to me, I mean to her —"

"Julie, focus," said Neal. He pointed to the hall. "In fact, everybody focus. Down the hall. Look!"

Eric gasped. "Holy cow. The real Dumpella!"

They turned to see a girl exactly like Julie, from her red cheeks to her pink shoes, tramp loudly into the room and over to the frozen duke.

"Snorfo, there you are! Well, your great and wonderful dukeyness of Ut, our visitor is finally here, but don't ask me to tell you his name because when I'm wearing these tight shoes, I can hardly remember my own name —"

She stopped and stared at the duke. Then she turned to the children. "Wait a second. What's going on here? Why is my brother all frozen up? And who are all of you? And, you, why are you wearing my clothes and — oh! — my *face*?"

Julie took a deep breath. "It's a long story," she said. "And I'm sorry I look like you, but we came to Ut to free our friend Hoja. He's a genie."

"We found him okay," added Eric, "but now we need to find our wizard friend —"

"Wizard?" said Dumpella. "With all the powers? That's who's here now! He's on his way to the palace to talk to my brother. But, gee, my brother is all so icy. . . ."

Max jumped. "Galen? My master? Did you see him? Where is he?"

Dumpella chewed her lip as if she were thinking. Then she tapped her foot. Finally, she shrugged. "Does Galen wear fish fins on his ears —"

Everyone gasped.

"Holy komoly!" cried Eric. "Lord Sparr is here?"

Dumpella jumped. "That's his name! And, boy, he brought a lot of chubby red men with him. Tell me, is he nice?"

The floor rumbled, shaking the glass cases.

"We're wasting time!" said Hoja. "If Sparr is here, something bad is going on. I must see what I can find out." Adjusting his turban, he darted out of the room and into the hallway.

"And I'll scout for Galen," said Max, scampering after him.

"Will somebody tell me what's going on?" asked Dumpella.

Eric looked at her standing next to Julie and suddenly smiled.

"Dumpella, it's complicated. But Sparr is not nice, and he's in Ut for a reason." He turned to his friends. "Guys, I know it might sound crazy, but there's one way to find out why Sparr is here and mess up his plans. . . ."

"Blast him good?" said Neal. *"Zzanng?"*

Eric shook his head. "No. At least not yet. Neal, you and Julie have to be the duke and his sister. You need to meet with Sparr."

"What?" said Neal. "Oh, no. No way. You're right, it does sound crazy. It *is* crazy. Sparr is, you know . . . Sparr! He'll hurt us bad. Really bad. Julie, help us out here —"

"I don't know," said Julie, chewing her lip. "These shoes really hurt. But . . ." She looked up at Neal's hair. "I guess a little gel would help."

"I have gel!" said Dumpella.

"Oh, please, no," he grumbled.

Keeah laughed. "Neal, if you play your part, Sparr will never know it's you. We'll find out why he's here and be able to trick *him* for once!"

"This sounds like fun," said Dumpella.

Hoja and Max hustled back from the doorway. "Ninns are marching into the palace. Well, if you want to call it marching. More like clomping. And Sparr is right behind them."

"But no Galen," said Max. "Not yet."

"We have a plan," said Dumpella.

"Which doesn't really include you," said Keeah. "I'm sorry."

"Maybe you can, well, hide until we're done," said Hoja.

"Good idea," said Eric. "Just long enough for us to stop Sparr, find Galen, and be off! Can you do that?"

"I guess," said Dumpella. "There is a secret place I go to when Snorfo gets too loud. I can go there." She turned.

"Wait," said Julie. "Before you go, I have to say that you really shouldn't let your brother boss you around."

"I shouldn't?" Dumpella said.

"No. Stand up for yourself. You're pretty much the duchess of Ut. Make a better home for your people. So that the next time Ut appears in Droon, it will be a nice place to visit."

Dumpella chewed her lip for a moment, then her eyes grew wide. "You know, you're right. Snorfo shouldn't boss me around. I'll do it!"

Julie gave her a hug. "And find better shoes."

"Tell me about it!" said Dumpella. "Okay, then, everyone. Good luck!"

"Thank you," said Keeah.

Dumpella clomped off through the halls and was gone.

Eric carefully pulled the iron glove from the frozen duke. "Come on. I saw costumes in the first room. They'll help us."

Minutes later, the troop gathered under the front archway of the museum. Together, they gazed out onto the sun-baked, blue-tiled square.

Neal looked exactly like the duke and Julie exactly like Dumpella. Keeah wore the mask with two noses, and Eric was dressed in a giant robe, with a long bushy mustache nearly covering his face.

It was already late in the afternoon.

"We have about an hour before Ut goes back into the bottle," said Keeah. "Let's hurry."

As they made their way across the hot square, Eric glanced at the tiles soaking up the sun. The earth rumbled once again, and he saw tiny cracks appear on the blue tiles in the center.

Eric . . . spoke a voice, silently, to him.

Instantly, he remembered Quill's words.

Whispers of doom.

Silently, he spoke back. **Who is that? Who's there?**

"My gosh, look!" said Julie, pointing.

In the distance they saw a figure in a blue robe, moving over the roof of a high building overlooking the square.

"It's Galen!" yelped Max. "I'd know him anywhere. Galen!"

The wizard was following a form in white cloth, spinning, whirling ahead of him, drawing him on over the rooftops.

"But who is that with him?" asked Julie.

Even from a distance, they could see that Galen was different. He stumbled as he ran, pausing as if he were tired, then continuing on.

"Galen?" cried Keeah.

As if he heard, the wizard stopped and stared down at Keeah for what seemed like a long time. At the sound of trumpets blaring above the palace walls, he turned again and made his way toward a higher roof.

"I will track him," said Hoja. "Max, come with me. The rest of you, remember

* 84 *

what the First Genie of the Dove once said. *'Plicky-wicky-frum-thrum!'"*

Keeah scratched her two noses. "What does that mean?"

Hoja laughed. "I haven't the faintest idea. But the genie also said, 'When in danger, protect what you love, for it will protect you!' Now, go!"

With that, the genie and the spider troll scurried up to the nearest rooftop and were gone.

The ground shuddered again, sending a long crack across the face of the flower.

Eric breathed in. "Galen said that Ut was a mystery to solve. I think it's getting deeper. And we have less and less time to figure it out. Come on."

Trumpets blared again as the four children rushed to the giant palace.

Taking a deep breath, Neal pushed

ahead of his friends. He stormed into the large, cheering throne room. He shouted at the top of his lungs. "Here comes the mighty one! And by that I mean — MEEEE!"

Pausing at the door, Julie glanced at Eric and Keeah, then sighed. "Oh, brother!"

Eight

Interview with a Sorcerer

Neal swished his robes as he pranced into the giant room with Julie. Keeah and Eric followed close behind.

"Snorfo!" woofed the dog-headed guards lining the walls on either side of the thrones.

Neal turned to Keeah as he plopped into his seat. "Oh, servant, use those big leaves to fan us, PLEASE!"

Keeah grumbled as she picked up a big

palm leaf. "Just don't get used to this, Neal. . . ."

"A little less noise there!" snorted Julie.

Eric saw that next to the thrones was a big globe of Droon. It was the second one he'd seen that day. A large yellow star marked where the city of Ut stood on the Saladian Plains.

The trumpets sounded once more, and an archway at the far end of the room suddenly became filled by the shoulders of three big Ninn warriors.

Eric . . . whispered the voice.

"And now —" grunted the largest Ninn, "make way for Lord Sparr —"

The room seemed to darken when the sorcerer stepped in. The fins behind his ears burned bright red. So did the scar on his forehead, marking where he was stung by his own Golden Wasp.

His black cloak shone like a raven's feathers.

As he strode forward, his cloak sweeping across the floor, the mysterious voice kept speaking silently in Eric's head.

Eric . . . it's nearly time! I'm . . . coming!

Shhhh! Eric hissed back.

Slowly, the sorcerer pulled up to the throne and stopped, his eyes narrowing at Neal.

"You look like someone . . . I know. . . ."

Neal had a bored look on his face. He looked at his fingernails, then tapped the throne's armrest with his metal glove. "*Flub-de-dub-dub . . .*"

The sorcerer's lips rose in a cruel smile. "But you seem much more agreeable — Duke of Ut!" Sparr made a deep bow, then looked Eric and Keeah up and down.

"Oh, don't mind these two," Julie said

to Sparr. "They're just our servants . . . Lunko and Bombo!"

Thanks a lot for the names, Keeah said silently to Julie. *Ask Sparr why he's here. What does he want?*

The floor shook slightly, and there were sudden cawing sounds from the flying groggles outside. Eric knew then that Sparr and his Ninns must have flown on them to Ut.

The sorcerer stepped closer to the thrones. "You are both probably wondering why I am here."

Neal shrugged. "You heard what a NIFTY PLACE I have! And you wanted to VISIT?"

Neal! Keeah said silently. *Don't be funny!*

Sparr lowered his gaze to the globe by the side of Julie's throne. He put his hand on it and gave it a push. All the seas and mountains, cities and deserts blurred as it spun around and around.

Eric stared at it. He had been seeing maps of Droon all day long. His heart began to pound.

Sparr stopped the globe, holding his finger on the yellow star. "Ut is a most unusual place," he said.

"Well, it's kept inside a bottle," said Julie. "That's unusual."

"And it is very important to me," said Sparr. "I have been waiting for so very many days. A hundred and eighty-seven days, to be exact —"

Eric gasped.

A hundred and eighty-seven days!

It was the same number of days since Eric had gained powers. Since Keeah had zapped him in the Doom Gate and he became a wizard.

He glanced at Keeah. She frowned. He knew she was trying to figure it out, too.

A hundred and eighty-seven days ago, they were all in the Serpent Sea, battling to imprison the Red Eye of Dawn into the Doom Gate.

Eric's heart kept thundering in his chest.

"I looked at my charts, consulted the sky, spun my own globe around on its axis," Sparr went on, turning the globe again. "Of course, I heard the rumbling and quaking of the earth. I saw the storms roar into the Serpent Sea. Then I learned of the bottle and of Ut, and I knew. It would be here."

What would be here? What?

The ground shook beneath the palace.

The sorcerer smiled. "My wait is over. I have come for what belongs to me. After one hundred and eighty-seven days, I shall have what I want, right from the center of your big blue flower."

Eric tried to recall what Quill had written about the blue flower.

The flower that booms.

He thought of the cracks across the blue design in the square outside. The rumbling. The quaking. The flower that . . . booms.

"And Droon will be mine. Droon, and the Upper World, too! Ninns, our time has come!"

Eric's blood ran cold. *This is crazy,* he spoke silently to Keeah. *Why Ut? Why here —*

We need to find Galen, replied Keeah. *Now.*

Eric tapped Neal and Julie lightly with the palm leaf. *Do everything you can to stall Sparr. Keep him here as long as you can. Keeah and I will meet you outside in ten minutes!*

Even as he bowed to Neal and edged away, Eric stared at the globe.

He thought of Hoja's map and of the magic globe turning and turning in the museum.

They all seemed to be saying the same thing.

Sparr spun the orb around slowly. Each time it revolved, Eric saw the Serpent Sea, the deserts of Lumpland, Jaffa City, the Saladian Plains. . . .

The Serpent Sea again . . . the Saladian Plains.

Keeah nudged Eric's arm. "It's time. Let's go!"

As Eric and Keeah crept to the back of the room, Neal rose from his throne.

"Before you go and get all powerful and stuff, Lord Sparr," he said, "how about WE PLAY A GAME?"

The fins behind Sparr's ears flashed deep red, almost black.

"What my brother means to say is . . ." said Julie, suddenly grabbing the globe from Sparr, "would you like a quick game of basketball?"

"What?" sneered Sparr.

Julie tossed up the globe, caught it, then threw it to Neal.

He grinned. "Yeah! First ten points takes it! You're not SCARED, are you, Sparr?"

Neal flung the ball to Sparr. It struck him in the chest.

Keeah slipped through the back curtain. "I can't watch."

"No," said Eric as he slid out onto a small balcony. "Besides, I think the real show will be down there in the square —"

Booom! One after another, tiles exploded from the square below. They flew straight up in the air and crashed to the ground in thousands of pieces.

Nine

The Yellow Star of Ut

Eric yanked off his mustache. "Let's find Galen."

Keeah tossed away her cloak and her mask. "If anyone can mix up Sparr, it's Neal. I wouldn't tangle with Julie, either. Come on, Bombo."

He stopped. "I thought you were Bombo."

"That makes you Lunko."

Eric frowned. "Never mind. Let's go!"

The two friends climbed over the balcony onto the palace roof, then down to the square.

As Keeah scanned the alleys for signs of Galen, Eric watched more and more tiles burst from the center of the square. Spirals of red flame shot up from the middle of the flower, while the whole ground shuddered.

Eric, I'm nearly here. . . .

The voice was louder now. Closer.

"Oh, my gosh, Eric!" gasped Keeah. "Look!"

He whirled around to see the bent figure of a man, his robe tattered and soiled, shuffling toward them down a narrow alley.

Eric's mouth dropped.

It was Galen, but as he'd never seen him before. The wizard was so very old. His hair was no more than wisps of white dangling from his head. His skin was deeply wrinkled and as pale as moonlight. His eyelids drooped over squinting eyes.

Galen looked as if he had aged a hundred years in a single day.

"How is this possible?" whispered Eric.

"There!" whispered Galen, pointing to a corner before them. "There . . . there!"

Eric turned.

And in the shadows he saw her.

It was a woman all in white. Eric couldn't tell whether she was old or young, but she was beautiful. Her hair hung to her shoulders in a thousand braids, each strand sparkling with innumerable tiny jewels.

Looking back at Eric, she seemed to silently speak a name to him. It was a name he'd heard before. Gasping, he spoke it aloud.

"Anusa!"

Her eyes met his for a second, then, as if she were no more than a ghost, she drifted back into the shadows soundlessly, a thing of smoke.

She was gone.

"It is Anusa!" said Galen. "I must follow her."

"Anusa? The genie?" said Keeah. "But, Galen, we need you now! You can't follow anyone. Sparr is here!"

Galen gazed into the princess's eyes. "Keeah, your great moment is nearly here. I will return for the battle to come. Until then, your love of Droon will guide you." His eyes lifted to the city wall in the distance. "As for today, some mysteries are no mystery at all. Sometimes, the truth is right before your eyes. Or under your feet. Anusa!"

Eric and Keeah turned to see the vision in white leaping along the top of the city wall. Even as they watched, the wizard vanished from where he was standing. He reappeared moments later on the distant wall, rushing after Anusa.

"Galen!" yelled Keeah. "I can't believe he's leaving us here. What are we going to do without him?"

"I don't know," said Eric. "I wish I could —"

Neal and Julie came rushing from the palace.

"Sparr's coming!" Neal yelled, out of breath.

"And he's a lousy sport!" shouted Julie, hobbling in her tall shoes. "He tried to blow up our globe!"

She tossed the globe of Droon to Eric.

And in that moment, everything came together. It was as if all that had happened that day finally made sense.

"I can't believe it," Eric said. "Sometimes the truth *is* right before your eyes!"

"What do you mean?" asked Keeah.

Eric held up the globe of Droon. "I know why Sparr came here today. He's gathering his three great Powers. He wants them all together."

The ground quaked again. A wave of heat rushed up from the earth.

"But what does it have to do with Ut?" asked Julie. "Sparr already has the Golden Wasp and the Coiled Viper. The Red Eye of Dawn is in the Doom Gate halfway around the world —"

Eric remembered how the Red Eye of Dawn, the blazing hot jewel, could control the forces of sky and water and earth.

The Red Eye created huge storms and fires.

And earthquakes.

"The Doom Gate *is* halfway around the world," said Eric. "Exactly halfway. It's like Hoja's note in the dungeon. If you can't escape — *you dig down*. It couldn't escape the Doom Gate by bursting out, so . . ."

Taking the globe, Eric held a finger on the Serpent Sea and another on the yellow star where Ut lay.

His fingers were pointing at each other.

"You mean the Eye isn't in prison?" asked Neal.

Ninns burst into the courtyard, clacking over the tiles toward the children.

"Not anymore," said Eric. "The Red Eye of Dawn burned all the way through the earth. It dug down from the Doom Gate and it's coming out here. Today. Right in Ut. That's why Sparr is here. He'll have his three Powers — Wait! There's Max!"

"Keeah, Eric!" The spider troll scurried to them from a nearby street. "I lost Hoja in the streets. But, I saw my master. Poor Galen, he was so old. Then he vanished!"

"We saw him, too," said Keeah. "He

said he had to follow the genie named Anusa —"

Booooom! More blue tiles shot up into the air, fell, and crashed at their feet.

Eric . . . get ready. . . .

"Enough!" said Eric. "All day I've been hearing a voice whispering of doom. Until now, I didn't know who it was. Now I do. It's Om. The spirit in the Red Eye of Dawn. He's . . . here —"

"So is he!" cried Neal. "Take a look. Here comes Sparr!"

As the ground heaved and quaked, Sparr marched into the square. "Ninns!" he yelled.

Pooom! The square rippled, sending more blue tiles buckling across the ground.

The earth shuddered. The palace shook. Tiles burst higher and higher, clattering to the street and crashing over the roofs of the city.

"My great plan!" cried Sparr. "Come to me, Om! Come, my Red Eye of Dawn! Come! Come!"

And it did come, bursting free from the earth, the great red jewel, the Red Eye of Dawn.

It blasted up with a terrific explosion, and the air filled with the whisperings of the dark spirit Om.

Free! it cried. *I am — FREE!*

Ten

The Urns Return

Sparr's eyes flashed bright red. The scar on his forehead deepened and looked almost fresh, just as it had when the Golden Wasp stung him.

"I have the Viper," he shouted. "I have the Wasp. No one can stop me from taking the Red Eye of Dawn, too!"

The gleaming jewel rose out of the broken earth and into the air over the square, shooting off bolts of red lightning.

"You want everything!" shouted Eric. "Then — take this. Keeah!"

Together, Eric and Keeah sent a powerful blast of wizard light at Sparr, their silver and blue sparks mingling in a giant bolt.

Kla-bammmm! The force of it blew the sorcerer to the ground.

Eric! Om whispered, and the jewel's flame leaped. *Eric —*

"Don't even start with me, gem boy!" Eric snarled. In a flash, he grabbed the duke's iron glove from Neal. Leaping up, he closed it around the blazing jewel.

Beams of light shot through the glove's iron fingers.

"No!" cried Sparr, staggering to his feet. "It's mine!"

"Everyone — let's go!" cried Keeah.

The kids shot into a narrow alley, heading for the wall. The Ninns charged, squeezing into the alley after them. The dog-faced guards barked loudly, then followed, waving their black nets. The children rushed up one street after another.

"They're closing in on us!" shouted Max.

"I have an idea," said Julie. "Neal, let's get rid of our stuff!"

She pulled off her tall pink shoes, while Neal clutched the Droon globe. At the count of three, they threw them at the first line of charging Ninns.

"Arghh!" Four red warriors tripped on the globe, while two others fell over the shoes. The troop of dog-headed guards couldn't stop in time.

"*Ooomph! Eeee! Ahhh! Woo-oof!*"

The Ninns and guards tumbled across the narrow alley.

"Yahoo! Traffic jam!" hooted Neal.

"Sparr is still coming!" cried Max. "Oh, I wish Galen were here!"

They raced around a corner into another street.

"Yikes!" said Eric. "Dead end. We're trapped. Sparr will find us."

"There's Hoja!" said Keeah.

The genie was at the end of the tiny street, licking what looked like mustard from his fingers and leaning on an urn of Parthnoop.

Everyone rushed to him.

"Hoja!" said Neal. "Why aren't you moving? Is that mustard? I mean, never mind! In a second we'll be trapped in Ut and thrown in a dungeon with no windows and be stuck there for a hundred years! With no food at all!"

The sound of Sparr's yelling grew louder.

Hoja twisted his turban slightly. "Yes, well, I just remembered what else these urns are good for," he said.

Hoisting himself up, he hopped inside one of them.

"Ahem! Urn of Parthnoop, please fly!"

The urn lifted up from the street with Hoja standing in it. "Now, unless you want to be, well, what Neal said, I suggest you pick a pot and hop in!"

The kids jumped into the urns and politely asked them to fly. *Whoosh!* All the urns of Parthnoop suddenly lifted from the ground just as a very angry group of Ninns and guards charged into the alley.

With a quick wave from Hoja — *voo-oo-oom!* — the urns shot up toward the purple walls of the city.

"Ya-HOO!" yelled Julie. "We are out of here!"

As they roared over the streets, Duke Snorfo came running from the Museum of Magic.

"Ah, yes," said Hoja, "that spell is over now."

"Get back here!" cried the duke, shaking a soft, pink fist at Neal.

"Sorry!" said Neal, turning his urn. "Ut's not big enough for both of us. You can have it. Bye!"

Dumpella poked her head out of a little window in the palace and waved. "Bye!"

Julie waved back. Then she noticed the Ninns mounting a group of groggles. "Uh-oh. Our problems aren't over yet!"

The air filled with the sound of groggles flapping noisily. In the midst of the flying lizards flew a great black one. On its back was Sparr himself.

Kaww! Kaww! the groggles called, darkening the air.

"They're gaining on us!" said Eric, still clutching the jewel in his glove. "Oh, my gosh. Look there. Galen. Galen!"

Looping their urns up over the streets, the friends caught a glimpse of the old wizard. He was standing on the very top of the city wall. A moment later, he vanished.

"Oh, dear, dear!" said Max. The urns lifted again and the Saladian Plains stretched out before them once more.

Sunset was coming fast, and still the groggles flapped closer.

"I have an idea," said Keeah. *"Pah-koom-la!"*

Instantly, the dunes whirled up from below, sending a dozen spinning funnels of sand high into the air.

Kroooo! the flying lizards howled. Then they coughed. Finally, they began to drop.

"Nooo!" yelled Sparr, as his groggle dipped back to earth. "The Red Eye of Dawn is mine! My jewel! The battle is not over, Eric Hinkle!"

"Too bad the groggles don't care!" shouted Julie.

In a mess of wings and tails, the flying lizards crashed and bumped one another. Finally, they veered away, turning to the Dark Lands.

"Yes!" cried Hoja. "And now to earth." He waved his arms, and the urns dropped into the sand — *thud-thud-thud!*

"It's time," said Keeah. "Follow me."

The small band raced behind the princess's airplane just as the sun dipped behind the western mountains.

Suddenly, the great purple walls of Ut seemed to move as if they were alive. The shapes and turns and angles of the city began to shiver.

"It's happening," said Julie.

A moment later — *pfffffft!* — the walls became smoke once again. The air grew thick and hazy, and the entire city — all its

buildings, creatures, people, everything —
went sweeping off the sands and back into
the bottle.

Sloooorp! The city was gone.

All that remained were a last few wisps
of smoke. Soon even they were gone.

Keeah grabbed the bottle from where it
lay tilted in the sand and quickly slapped
the cork back in it. "And that's that!" she
said.

Before them, the dune was only a
mound of sand, with almost nothing to
show that a giant purple city had stood
there moments before.

Almost nothing.

In the sand, where the highest purple
wall had stood, was a slender trail of footprints.

Max rushed to it, got on his knees, and
counted. "Two sets of footprints!" he said.

"Anusa," said Eric. He told Hoja what

he and Keeah had seen of the mysterious genie.

"So!" said Hoja. "He found Anusa. She lured him away with her."

"Look here," said Max, pointing at the ground. "As if wings blew down on the grains of sand, the footprints vanish at this point! My Galen . . . he's . . . gone."

Keeah shook her head. "He's on an adventure. It's like Quill wrote. *Fly me up, you flying dove. Fair as the moon, the one I love.* Galen lost Anusa long ago, but he found her again."

"He said he would come back," said Eric.

Max looked up at the darkening sky. The first stars began to appear. He quivered, then he smiled. "He *will* be back. Stronger than ever. With lots to tell. I know he will. We must be ready for him!"

"We will be," said Keeah. She put her

arm around the spider troll, hugging him tight.

Eric looked in the iron glove. The many-faceted crimson jewel lay in his palm, silent for now. "The Red Eye of Dawn doesn't seem so fierce now," he said. "And neither does Sparr."

The only sign of the sorcerer was the black trail of groggles streaking toward the Dark Lands in the distance.

"He's got two Powers, but not the third," said Julie.

"Yeah, I'd say we scored a three-pointer today," said Neal.

Together, Keeah and Max took the jewel and glove from Eric and dropped them in a small box on the *Dragonfly*.

Eric remembered Sparr's last words.

The battle is not over.

He turned the words over in his head.

"The battle isn't over," he said aloud.

"But I think that's why we're here. To protect what we love. To help win that battle."

"And we shall do it," said Hoja. "All of you go where you must. My mission was to find the genie Anusa. She's not in Ut anymore, but I still have that mission. Perhaps I shall find Galen in the bargain. Good-bye, then!"

"Good luck!" chirped Max.

The genie followed the footprints in the sand. When he got to where they ended, he wiggled his turban and faded away like a scent in the air.

"Our time to go, too," said Julie. She pointed to the rainbow stairs glistening on the crest of a nearby hill.

Everyone piled into the plane. Taking the wheel, Keeah zoomed it right up to the hill. The bottom step of the staircase seemed to float in midair as the plane pulled alongside it.

Keeah smiled at her friends. "Until next time. I know I won't have to wait very long!"

Eric nodded. "We'll be here in a flash."

"I've got only one thing to add," said Neal with a laugh. *"Plicky-wicky-frum-thrum!"*

The kids hugged, then Eric, Neal, and Julie jumped to the stairs.

Looking once more at the great Saladian Plains, empty and quiet as before, they raced up the stairs to Eric's house.

At the top, Julie closed the door on Droon, then turned to Neal. "After watching you play the duke today, I don't think I'll ever look at you the same way."

"I think that could be a good thing," Neal said with a grin. "But the best part is that we stopped Sparr, got the Red Eye of Dawn, played dress-up, and flew in magical urns, all before breakfast!"

Eric laughed as he charged up to the kitchen with his friends. "It's like I said this morning: Today is going to be a great day!"